THUNDERSTORM

Mary Szilagyi

Bradbury Press / New York

Bradbury Press, an Affiliate of Macmillan, Inc., 866 Third Avenue, New York, N.Y. 10022 Collier Macmillan Canada, Inc. Manufactured in the United States of America 10 9 8 7 6 5 4 3 2 1 The text of this book is set in 16 pt. Galliard. The illustrations are colored-pencil drawings, reproduced in full color.

Library of Congress Cataloging in Publication Data: Szilagyi, Mary. Thunderstorm. Summary: A little girl is comforted by her mother during a thunderstorm and she in turn comforts the family dog. 1. Children's stories, American. [1. Thunderstorms—Fiction. 2. Fear—Fiction] I. Title PZ7.S989Th 1985 [E] 84-24570
ISBN 0-02-788580-1

To Catherine

The sun is shining.
The little girl is busy,
filling the wagon with sand from the sandbox.

The dog is watching.

Now she is taking the sand
to build a hill in a hole by the tree
at the edge of the garden.
The wagon is heavy, and the day is still.

Something moves.

A rustle flattens the leaves of the tree.
A bird calls to another bird that a storm is coming.

The sky is light.

The little girl looks up.

She listens.

Yes, she hears a crackle far away,
high in the sky—the beginning of thunder.

She runs to the house, crying.

She finds her mother, who knows
she is afraid of storms.
"You are safe here," says her mother.
"We will watch the storm together."

Still the little girl cries.

The dog at the door scratches to come inside.

Thick drops hit the grass.
The trees bend and roll. The sky is dark.

The little girl moves closer to her mother.

The dog hides.

The storm crashes and flashes
and rumbles outside.

CRACK!

FLASH!

Where is the dog?

The little girl hears panting.
The dog is still hiding.

The little girl pats the dog,
who crawls close.
"You are safe here," she says.

The dog trembles.

BOOM!

SPLASH!

The mother and the little girl
and the dog sit close.
Soon the lightning ends,
and the sound of thunder softens.

Now it is just raining.

The rain falls on the grass and on the sandbox
and on the wagon full of sand.
Leaves have fallen from the tree,
like scraps of the storm.

The rain stops, and the sound of thunder
is far, far away.

The dog stops shaking.
The little girl remembers that she cried.

The sun is shining.

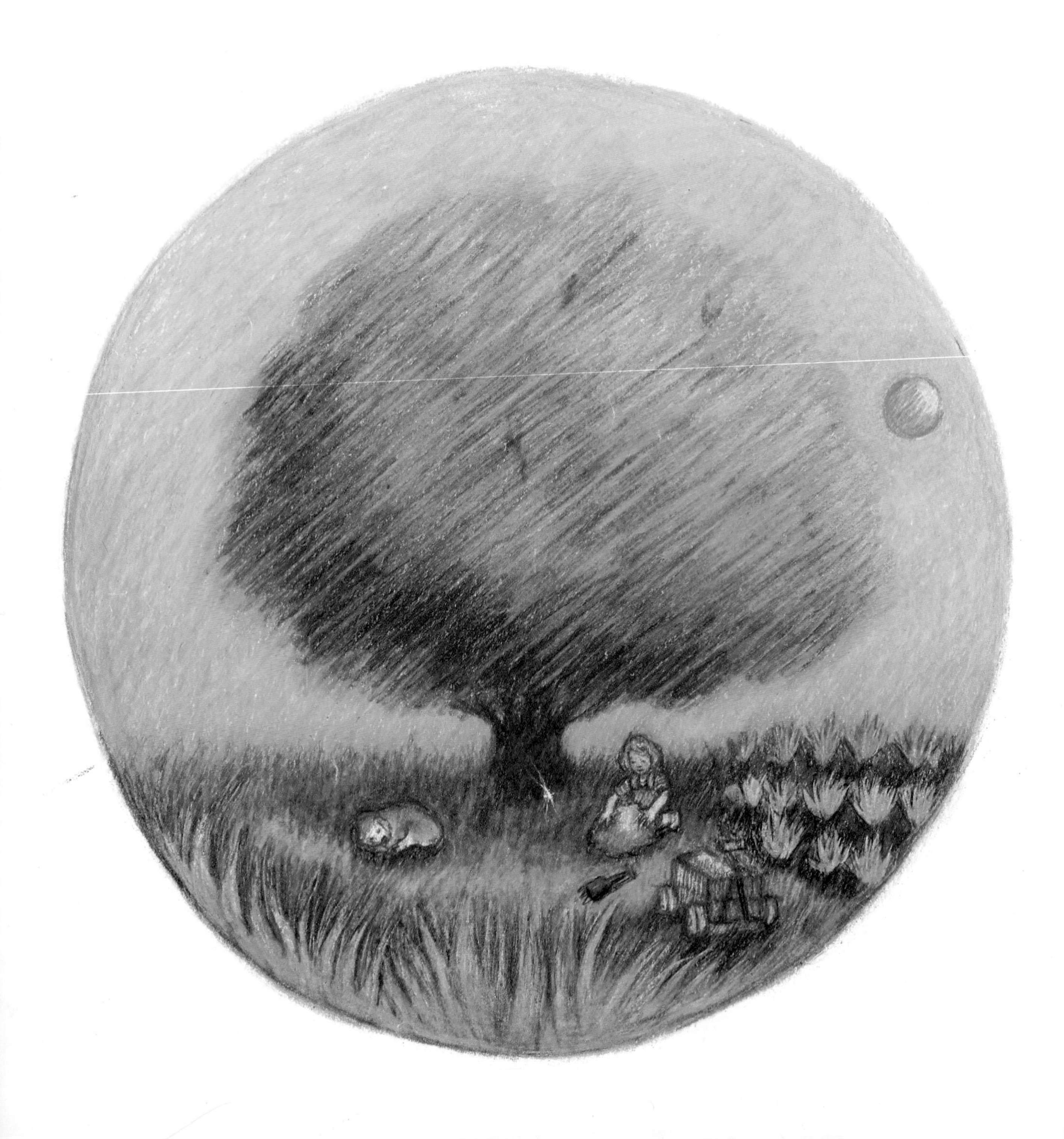